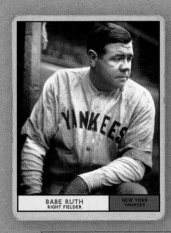

BABE RUTH
RIGHT FIELDER

NEW YORK
YANKEES

MICKEY MANTLE
LEFT FIELDER

NEW YORK
YANKEES

THE STORY OF THE NEW YORK YANKEES

Published by Creative Education
P.O. Box 227, Mankato, Minnesota 56002
Creative Education is an imprint of The Creative Company
www.thecreativecompany.us

Design and production by Blue Design
Art direction by Rita Marshall
Printed by Corporate Graphics in the United States of America

Photographs by Getty Images (Ron Antonelli/NY Daily News Archive, Al Bello, Diamond Images, Focus on Sport, Charles Franklin/MLB Photos, Leon Halip, Jed Jacobsohn/Allsport, Keystone, Kidwiler Collection/Diamond Images, Edwin Levick/Hulton Archive, Jim McIsaac, National Baseball Hall of Fame Library/MLB Photos, NY Daily News Archive, Hy Peskin/Time & Life Pictures, Rich Pilling/MLB Photos, Photo File/MLB Photos, Arthur Rickerby/Diamond Images, Robert Riger, Mark Rucker/Transcendental Graphics, Jamie Squire, Mike Theiler/AFP)

Library of Congress Cataloging-in-Publication Data

Goodman, Michael E.
The story of the New York Yankees / by Michael E. Goodman.
p. cm. — (Baseball: the great American game)
Includes index.
Summary: The history of the New York Yankees professional baseball team from its inaugural 1903 season to today, spotlighting the team's greatest players and most memorable moments.
ISBN 978-1-60818-049-3
1. New York Yankees (Baseball team)—History—Juvenile literature. I. Title. II. Title: New York Yankees. III. Series.

GV875.N4G66 2011
796.357'64097471—dc22   2010025210

CPSIA: 110310 PO1381

First Edition
9 8 7 6 5 4 3 2 1

Page 3: Center fielder Joe DiMaggio
Page 4: First baseman Mark Teixeira

BASEBALL: THE GREAT AMERICAN GAME

THE STORY
OF THE
NEW YORK
YANKEES

Michael E. Goodman

CONTENTS

HIGH ON A HILL

In 1626, Dutch businessman Peter Minuit paid leaders of the Canarsee Indian tribe $24 in beads and cloth to purchase a small island along America's Atlantic coast, where he established the colony of New Amsterdam. The Indians called the island *manna hatta*, meaning "many hills." In the 1660s, the British took over the colony and renamed it New York, but the island retained its Indian name, Manhattan. Today, Manhattan is the richest and most important part of New York City and the home of America's main financial institutions, best-known theaters and museums, and most crowded city streets.

In 1903, Manhattan also became the home of one of the first teams in professional baseball's new American League (AL). Because the club played its games at Hilltop Park, atop one of Manhattan's highest hills, it was originally called the New York Highlanders. Some sportswriters thought that name was too long and cumbersome, however, so they often used "Yankees" in their newspaper headlines. When the club moved to another field in a lower locale, "Highlanders" didn't seem appropriate

Night or day, the streets of New York always seem to be bright and bustling, which explains its nickname, "The City that Never Sleeps."

PITCHER · WHITEY FORD

Edward "Whitey" Ford dominated AL batters with guile rather than power. He could deliver any of four pitches—fastball, slider, curveball, or sinker—from a variety of arm angles, so a hitter never knew exactly what was coming. And the more important the game, the better he performed. Said Yankees outfielder Mickey Mantle, "I don't care what the situation was, how high the stakes were—the bases could be loaded and the pennant riding on every pitch, it never bothered Whitey. He pitched his game. He had nerves of steel." Ford still holds World Series career pitching records for most starts (22), wins (10), and strikeouts (94).

WHITEY FORD
PITCHER

NEW YORK YANKEES

STATS

Yankees seasons: 1950, 1953–67

Height: 5-foot-10

Weight: 180

- **236–106 career record**
- **.690 career winning percentage**
- **8-time All-Star**
- **Baseball Hall of Fame inductee (1974)**

Highlanders star Jack Chesbro's 41 pitching wins in 1904 set a major-league record that will probably stand forever.

JACK CHESBRO

anymore. So, in 1913, the team officially became known as the Yankees.

The early Highlanders clubs were led on offense by 5-foot-4, spray-hitting outfielder "Wee Willie" Keeler and on the mound by iron-armed pitcher Jack Chesbro. In 1904, Chesbro pitched a remarkable 455 innings and won 41 games. But his season will always be remembered for the ninth wild pitch he threw that year. It occurred on the last day of the season and cost the Highlanders a chance to win their first AL pennant.

The Yankees struggled in their early years until Miller Huggins took over as manager in 1918. Over the next 12 seasons, Huggins would lead the club to 6 AL pennants and 3 World Series titles. Huggins constructed one of the most powerful lineups in baseball history, a batting order known as "Murderers' Row." At the center of Murderers' Row was barrel-chested, thin-legged Babe Ruth, whose ability to hit home runs revolutionized the way baseball was played. Before Ruth came along, players hit home runs almost by accident. But the Babe swung from his heels, looking to blast the ball out of the park. He put so much effort into his swing that fans were thrilled even if he missed. When he connected, however, the effect on the crowd was almost magical.

Ruth joined the Yankees in 1920 via a deal with the Boston Red Sox and quickly became the most popular athlete in America. Ruth's skills and popularity convinced the Yankees to build a bigger stadium in the Bronx, across the Harlem River from Manhattan. On opening day in 1923, 74,000 enthusiastic fans packed the new Yankee Stadium, mostly to watch Ruth. They weren't disappointed; the "Bambino" smacked a home run to win the game. He would end his first year at Yankee Stadium with a .393 batting average, 41 homers, and 131 runs batted in (RBI).

Ruth was joined on Murderers' Row in 1923 by another superstar: first baseman Lou Gehrig. Other sluggers in the lineup included outfielder Bob Meusel and second baseman Tony Lazzeri. The Yankees claimed their first world championship in 1923. That was followed by titles in 1927, 1928, and 1932. After Ruth retired in 1934, Gehrig starred on four more Yankees championship teams during the 1930s.

LOU GEHRIG

NEW YORK FASHION

Today's professional baseball players wear colorful uniforms complete with artistic logos, numerals, and nameplates. But in baseball's earliest days, uniforms were much plainer. Then, in 1912, the Yankees decided to jazz up their bland white shirts and pants with black pinstripes. The new look delighted fans, who felt that their players dressed classier than any other team's, even if they didn't win that often. Pinstripes have been a key part of the Yankees' look ever since. By 1929, the Yankees were the best team in baseball, and team management decided to make another uniform change to show off the members

of "Murderers' Row." That year, the Yanks became the first team to include permanent numbers on the backs of players' shirts. The numbers were assigned according to batting order, so because Babe Ruth and Lou Gehrig batted third and fourth, they wore numbers 3 and 4, respectively. There was no need to put the players' names on the back; fans recognized all of the Yankees' sluggers by appearance and playing style. Even today, Yankees uniforms have no names sewn on. The Yankees were also the first team to retire players' numbers, including those of Ruth, Gehrig, and 14 other baseball immortals.

CATCHER · YOGI BERRA

Today, Lawrence "Yogi" Berra is known primarily for the mind-bending comments he would frequently make, such as, "It's tough to make predictions, especially about the future" or "It ain't over 'til it's over." But during the 1950s, Berra was the glue that held the Yankees' dynasty together. Berra didn't look like a great athlete. He was short and stocky, but he generated amazing power as a hitter and showed great agility as a catcher. "He seemed to be doing everything wrong, yet everything came out right," said New York Giants outfielder Mel Ott. "He stopped everything behind the plate and hit everything in front of it."

YOGI BERRA
CATCHER

NEW YORK
YANKEES

STATS

Yankees seasons: 1946–63

Height: 5-foot-7

Weight: 195

- **1,430 career RBI**

- **3-time AL MVP**

- **15-time All-Star**

- **Baseball Hall of Fame inductee (1972)**

THE BABE CALLS HIS SHOT

Babe Ruth's feats on the ballfield inspired legends. One of the most famous involves an at bat during Game 3 of the 1932 World Series against the Chicago Cubs. As the game began, Chicago players and fans screamed insults at Ruth, calling him fat and washed-up. Ruth temporarily silenced them in the first inning when he smacked a pitch by Cubs hurler Charley Root into the right-field stands to put the Yankees ahead, 3–0. In the fourth inning, when the Babe botched a play in right field that allowed the Cubs to tie the game, the fans were ecstatic. The catcalls grew louder when Ruth came to bat in the fifth. The slugger took two strikes; then he stuck out his arm and pointed. Was he pointing toward the pitcher or toward Wrigley Field's center-field stands? No one is quite sure. But Ruth smashed the next pitch over the fence in the general direction in which he had been pointing. The next day, New York reporters wrote that Ruth had "called his shot," showing where he would hit the pitch. Smiling, Ruth backed up the reporters' version. Because the story involved the Babe, most fans believed it happened just that way.

BABE RUTH

Murderers' Row members Babe Ruth (second from left) and Bob Meusel (second from right) along with (from left) first baseman Wally Pipp, shortstop Roger Peckinpaugh, and third baseman Frank "Home Run" Baker.

If Ruth was spectacular, Gehrig was steady. "Lou Gehrig never learned that a ballplayer couldn't be good every day," said catcher Hank Gowdy of the rival New York Giants. Gehrig was always in the lineup and always ready to perform. Between June 1, 1925, and April 30, 1939, Gehrig played in 2,130 consecutive contests, a record that lasted until Baltimore Orioles shortstop Cal Ripken Jr. surpassed it in 1995. What finally stopped his streak was an incurable muscle disease called amyotrophic lateral sclerosis (ALS), which is still known as "Lou Gehrig's Disease."

JOLTIN' JOE AND THE MICK

Near the end of Gehrig's career, center fielder Joe DiMaggio arrived in New York. The quiet DiMaggio led his teammates more by example than by emotion. "He did things so easily," said Yankees catcher Bill Dickey, "people didn't realize how good he was." DiMaggio conducted himself with such grace on and off the field that reporters began calling him "The Yankee Clipper," after the elegant sailing ships.

DiMaggio's career in New York lasted 13 years, and during that time, the Yanks won an incredible 11 pennants and 10 World Series. DiMaggio twice topped the AL in home runs, won two batting titles, and captured three Most Valuable Player (MVP) awards—all impressive feats. But what he accomplished in 1941 was truly remarkable. That season, "Joltin' Joe" recorded at least 1 hit in 56 consecutive games, a record no other major-league player has come close to equaling. "The 1941 streak was

Joe DiMaggio and Mickey Mantle (pictured) were both superbly well-rounded, but Mantle packed more punch, hitting some monstrous home run blasts.

MICKEY MANTLE

THE STREAK

During the summer of 1941, Americans' minds were focused on two subjects: what Adolf Hitler's army was doing in Europe and whether Joe DiMaggio's hitting streak was still going strong. Starting on May 15, the center fielder recorded at least 1 hit every game for 2 months, for 56 games in all. (Previously, the longest streak had been 41 games, by first baseman George Sisler of the St. Louis Browns in 1922.) As a 1941 article in *TIME* magazine noted, "In 102 years of baseball, few feats have caused such nationwide to-do. Joe's hits have been the biggest news in U.S. sport." Even radio programs were interrupted to announce that DiMaggio had just gotten a hit. DiMaggio had a few close calls during the streak, sometimes failing to get a hit until his last at bat. Although the pressure was intense, "Joltin' Joe" always seemed composed on the outside. "But that doesn't mean I wasn't dying inside," he later confided to reporters. The streak finally ended on July 17 in Cleveland against the Indians. During those 56 games, DiMaggio batted a remarkable .408 with 15 homers. More importantly, the Yankees' record during the streak was 42–14, and they soon captured another AL pennant.

an unbelievable thing—day after day," recalled Yankees Hall of Fame shortstop Phil Rizzuto. "I don't think he got a soft hit the entire 56 games."

With DiMaggio leading the way—and supported by All-Star performers such as Rizzuto, clutch-hitting outfielder Tommy Henrich, and hard-throwing pitchers Allie Reynolds and Vic Raschi—the Yankees seemed invincible throughout the 1940s and into the next decade. The club won five straight world championships between 1949 and 1953 and continued its remarkable run of winning seasons. In fact, the Yanks would finish above .500 every season between 1926 and 1964.

As DiMaggio's career was ending in 1951, 19-year-old rookie outfielder Mickey Mantle arrived in New York. Mantle was a switch hitter who could belt mammoth home runs from both sides of the plate. Yankees manager Casey Stengel once remarked, "There are some who say he hits with more power right-handed, and there are others who say he hits with more power left-handed. They can't make up their minds. Now, wouldn't you say that was amazing?"

Mantle, who inherited the prized center field spot from DiMaggio in 1952, had a unique blend of speed, power, and desire. But he was not the

FIRST BASEMAN · LOU GEHRIG

Lou Gehrig once said of himself, "I'm just the guy who's in there every day, the fellow who follows Babe Ruth in the order." Yet Gehrig struck just as much fear into the hearts of AL pitchers as his more-famous teammate. The "Iron Horse" was an RBI machine, driving in 150 or more runs 7 times in his career. Gehrig earned the respect of New York fans for his courage and consistency, and when more than 61,000 turned out to honor him after he was forced to retire in 1939, the dying hero famously said, "Today I consider myself the luckiest man on the face of the earth."

LOU GEHRIG
FIRST BASEMAN

NEW YORK
YANKEES

STATS

Yankees seasons: 1923–39

Height: 6 feet

Weight: 200

- 493 career HR

- 1,995 career RBI

- 7-time All-Star

- Baseball Hall of Fame inductee (1939)

only star in the Yankees lineup. Other Yankees greats of that era included pitcher Whitey Ford and catcher Yogi Berra—both of whom would later join Mantle in the Hall of Fame. These players helped the Yankees win eight AL pennants and six world championships during the 1950s.

Unfortunately, Mantle's career was hampered by injuries. No one knows what records he might have set had he stayed healthy. In 1961, for example, Mantle and fellow Yankees outfielder Roger Maris were both challenging Babe Ruth's hallowed record of 60 home runs in a season. Then Mantle was slowed by a virus and hip infection. Maris eventually broke the record on the last day of the season, while Mantle—despite his health problems—managed to finish with a career-high 54 homers. "Nobody else would have played [with injuries like Mantle's]. Nobody," said Yankees catcher Elston Howard. "But Mickey wasn't like normal people."

Mantle led New York to three more pennants in 1962, 1963, and 1964. Then the team and its star began to fade. The Yanks hit rock bottom in 1966, finishing in 10th place in the league, and it would take a decade before they challenged for another AL pennant.

REBUILDING WITH THE BOSS

In 1973, shipping magnate George Steinbrenner bought the Yankees franchise and began rebuilding it. Steinbrenner, whose nickname in New York was "The Boss," became famous for two things: spending money freely on talented players and criticizing his high-priced acquisitions if they didn't perform as well as he expected them to.

Among The Boss's first significant moves were the signings of two free agents: control pitcher Jim "Catfish" Hunter and slugging outfielder Reggie Jackson. These stars combined with other talented players in New York—including gritty catcher Thurman Munson, slick-fielding third baseman Graig Nettles, crafty left-handed hurler Ron Guidry, and flamethrowing relief pitcher Rich "Goose" Gossage—to create a rising AL power.

The atmosphere in Yankee Stadium became electric in the late 1970s as the team began to win again. The air in the clubhouse was more volatile, though, as players screamed at each other, hot-tempered manager Billy Martin, and their owner. "Some kids dream of joining the

SECOND BASEMAN · JOE GORDON

"Joe Gordon was an acrobat. He was always in front of the ball," said Cleveland Indians Hall of Fame pitcher Bob Feller. Gordon fielded balls no other infielder would even try to reach and led all AL second basemen in assists in four different seasons. An excellent clutch hitter, Gordon played exactly 1,000 games for the Yankees and collected exactly 1,000 hits. He also had surprising power and still holds the AL record for career homers by a second-sacker. Gordon played in five World Series during his seven seasons with the Yankees, and he later helped lead the Indians to a World Series triumph in 1948.

JOE GORDON
SECOND BASEMAN

NEW YORK YANKEES

STATS

Yankees seasons: 1938–43, 1946

Height: 5-foot-10

Weight: 180

- 253 career HR

- 1942 AL MVP

- 9-time All-Star

- Baseball Hall of Fame inductee (2009)

THIRD BASEMAN · GRAIG NETTLES

During his career in New York, Graig Nettles rivaled the Baltimore Orioles' Brooks Robinson as the AL's top third baseman on both defense and offense. In the field, Nettles made spectacular diving stops to turn sure doubles into outs. Then, at bat, the left-handed slugger sent balls soaring over the right-field fence in Yankee Stadium; Nettles still holds the AL career record for homers by a third-sacker. In 1977, the two-way star earned a Gold Glove award for his fielding while slamming 37 homers, driving in 107 runs, and scoring 99 runs to lead the Yankees to their first world championship in 15 years.

STATS

Yankees seasons: 1973–83

Height: 6 feet

Weight: 185

- **390 career HR**
- **1,314 career RBI**
- **6-time All-Star**
- **2-time Gold Glove winner**

GRAIG NETTLES
THIRD BASEMAN

NEW YORK
YANKEES

REGGIE JACKSON

circus, others of becoming a major league baseball player," said Nettles. "As a member of the New York Yankees, I've gotten to do both."

In 1976, the Yankees topped the AL Eastern Division (the major leagues had been split into two divisions each in 1969) and won their first pennant in 12 years before being swept by the Cincinnati Reds' "Big Red Machine" lineup in the World Series. The next year, Jackson made sure they didn't lose. He blasted a major-league-record five home runs in the 1977 World Series, including three in the sixth and final game, to lead New York back to the top of the baseball world. When Jackson powered the Yanks to another championship in 1978, Steinbrenner crowned him "Mr. October," since Jackson always played his best in the postseason games of autumn.

YANKEES

After the Yankees lost the 1981 World Series, they slid downhill for the rest of the decade. The most consistent Yankees player during the 1980s was first baseman Don Mattingly, whose strong bat and remarkable fielding ability earned him the nickname "Donnie Baseball." Mattingly brought an intense attitude to the ballpark every day. "Check Donnie's eyes during a game," said Yankees pitcher Bob Tewksbury. "They're right out of a horror movie. He yells at opposing players. He paces in the dugout. I've never seen anyone compete with that kind of passion." Mattingly won the AL batting title in 1984 and was named the league's MVP in 1985. He also consistently earned Gold Glove awards as the AL's top-fielding first-sacker. Unfortunately, back problems robbed him of his power and mobility during much of the last half of his career.

Despite Mattingly's fine play and that of slugging outfielder Dave Winfield, The Boss became unhappy, as the Yankees missed the playoffs every year from 1982 to 1994. "For a lot of clubs, 13 years without being in the postseason is no big deal," said Steinbrenner. "But for the New York Yankees, it is unacceptable."

Determined to build another winner, the owner took a good look at his team before the 1995 season began. His roster featured Mattingly,

DON MATTINGLY

All-Star third baseman Wade Boggs, steady right fielder Paul O'Neill, and budding superstar center fielder Bernie Williams. The Boss added strength to the mound by signing pitcher David Cone and bringing up lefty Andy Pettitte from the minor leagues.

New York finished second in the AL East in 1995, earning the league's first-ever Wild Card berth in the playoffs. Unfortunately, the team's 1995 postseason stay would be short, as New York fell in five tight games to the Seattle Mariners in the first round. Following the season, Mattingly retired. Fans were saddened to see their hero go, but a new generation of Yankees was about to build a dynasty.

FOUR TITLES UNDER TORRE

Before the 1996 season began, Steinbrenner hired veteran manager and native New Yorker Joe Torre to assume leadership in the dugout. With his calm demeanor and vast baseball experience, Torre was the perfect choice to run the team and deal with The Boss. As one of his first moves, Torre inserted rookie shortstop Derek Jeter into the starting lineup. "The kid is ready," Torre declared. "It's time for him to earn his keep."

Jeter quickly proved that he was up to the task. The lanky, 6-foot-3 shortstop smacked his first major-league homer on opening day and kept on hitting throughout the year, easily earning AL Rookie of the Year honors. Adding Jeter and Panamanian relief ace Mariano Rivera in 1996 helped transform the Yankees from a talented team into a dominant one. In the playoffs that year, they defeated the Texas Rangers

Mariano Rivera was famous for his nasty cutter pitch—a fastball that curved as it reached the plate, often jamming batters and breaking bats.

SHORTSTOP · DEREK JETER

When he was only five, Derek Jeter told friends that he would someday play shortstop for the New York Yankees. Sixteen years later, he was doing just that, but his baseball career didn't get off to a great start. Drafted out of high school by the Yankees in 1992, Jeter committed 56 errors in his second minor-league season. Then, with endless practice and strong determination, he made himself into a Gold Glove fielder and an outstanding clutch hitter. "I work extremely hard," Jeter explained. "I like to be in the middle of things, and I'm not afraid to fail."

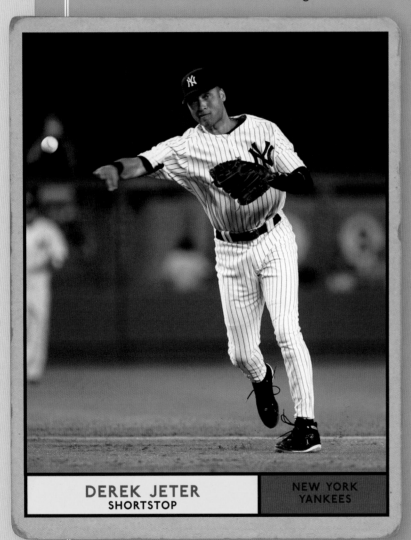

DEREK JETER
SHORTSTOP

NEW YORK
YANKEES

STATS

Yankees seasons: 1995–present

Height: 6-foot-3

Weight: 195

- **.314 career BA**

- **11-time All-Star**

- **1996 AL Rookie of the Year**

- **7 seasons of 200-plus hits**

THE ONE-GAME SEASON

For Yankees fans, the 1978 season was magical. That year, the Yanks made the greatest comeback in baseball history and left their hated rivals, the Boston Red Sox, feeling robbed again. The Yankees had a slow and uneasy start, while the Red Sox were flying high. On July 19, New York trailed Boston in the AL East by 14 games; no team had ever overcome that large a deficit. But after contentious manager Billy Martin was fired, the Yankees calmed down under new skipper Bob Lemon and found their focus. The Yanks started winning regularly and slowly closed the gap with Boston. The clubs ended the season deadlocked at 99–63 and facing a one-game playoff in Boston's Fenway Park to decide which would advance to the postseason. Boston struck first and led 2–0 going into the seventh inning. Then the Yankees' weak-hitting shortstop, Bucky Dent, confounded everyone by lofting a three-run homer over the "Green Monster" (Fenway's left-field wall) to put the Yankees ahead. New York held on for a 5–4 win. Boston fans, who still hated the Yankees for taking Babe Ruth from them in 1920, couldn't believe the 1978 pennant had been "stolen" as well.

LEFT FIELDER · MICKEY MANTLE

Mickey Mantle was destined to become a professional baseball player. Mantle's father named him "Mickey" after his favorite ballplayer, Hall of Fame catcher Mickey Cochrane of the Detroit Tigers. Mutt Mantle also trained his son to be a switch hitter, believing this skill would give him an edge over other players. He was right; during his 18-year career in New York, Mantle batted over .300 ten times and twice topped the 50-homer mark. Although he primarily played center field, following in the footsteps of Joe DiMaggio, Mantle used his outstanding speed and defensive skills to track balls down all over the outfield.

STATS

Yankees seasons: 1951–68

Height: 5-foot-11

Weight: 200

- 536 career HR

- 3-time AL MVP

- 16-time All-Star

- Baseball Hall of Fame inductee (1974)

MICKEY MANTLE
LEFT FIELDER

NEW YORK
YANKEES

and Baltimore Orioles to win the AL pennant and then took on the NL champion Atlanta Braves in the World Series. The Braves won the first two games before the Yanks turned the tables, taking the next four contests to capture their first world championship in 18 years. The Yankees had given notice—they were back.

In 1997, the Yanks made the playoffs again but were eliminated in the first round by the Cleveland Indians. That proved to be just a minor setback. The next three seasons, New York dominated major league baseball, capturing three straight AL pennants and then winning three consecutive World Series. Yankees fans got a special thrill in 2000, when their team outdueled its crosstown rival, the New York Mets, to earn its 26th title. That title meant that the Yankees had won more world championships than any other team in any other professional sport.

Jeter sparked the Yankees all 3 championship years, pounding out more than 200 hits each season. "Jeter gets better every year—that's what's remarkable about him," said broadcaster Ed Bradley during a profile on the shortstop on the television show *60 Minutes*. "Some guys are good and stay good. Some guys are good and get better. . . . It's that way with the best, whatever the profession. That's the way this kid is."

The Yankees were riding high as the new millennium began. To maintain the club's level of excellence, Steinbrenner outbid other owners to acquire free agents to fill gaps on the team. All-Star pitchers Mike Mussina and Roger Clemens joined the starting corps, and hard-hitting outfielder Gary Sheffield and slugging first baseman Jason Giambi added long-ball power to the Yanks' lineup. The Yankees even reached all the way around the world to entice outfielder Hideki Matsui, a Japanese legend, to come aboard their express train.

After all the free-agent signings, the Yankees' yearly payroll far exceeded that of every other team in baseball. Fans in other cities complained loudly that such a gap in payrolls gave New York an unfair advantage, and they labeled the Yankees "The Evil Empire." Yankees fans dismissed such comments as jealousy and were delighted that their franchise was willing to spend more money if it meant more championships.

HIDEKI MATSUI

CENTER FIELDER · JOE DiMAGGIO

"The Yankee Clipper" was more than just a great ballplayer; he was a legend. Tall, handsome, graceful, and reserved, DiMaggio never seemed flustered or out of control—on or off the field. Said Yankees catcher Bill Dickey, "He was a guy who knew he was the greatest baseball player in America, and he was proud of it. He knew what the press and fans and kids expected of him, and he was always trying to live up to that image." In a nationwide poll conducted during Major League Baseball's 100th anniversary in 1969, DiMaggio easily topped the voting as the sport's "greatest living player."

JOE DiMAGGIO
CENTER FIELDER

NEW YORK
YANKEES

STATS

Yankees seasons: 1936–42, 1946–51

Height: 6-foot-2

Weight: 193

- **.325 career BA**

- **3-time AL MVP**

- **13-time All-Star**

- **Baseball Hall of Fame inductee (1955)**

The Yankees seemed on their way to championship number 27 in early September 2001. Then, on September 11, everything in New York changed when the city's World Trade Center was destroyed by terrorists, and nearly 3,000 people were killed. Baseball was put on hold while the city and the country attempted to recover. When play resumed, so did the Yankees' pennant drive. They won the AL East again, then knocked off the Oakland A's and Seattle Mariners in the playoffs to earn a berth in the World Series opposite the Arizona Diamondbacks.

In one of the most exciting and emotional World Series of all time, the two teams battled through seven tense contests. In the bottom of the ninth inning of Game 7, the Yankees held a 2–1 lead, and closer Mariano Rivera was on the mound in Arizona's Chase Field. Throughout New York's dominant run in the late '90s, Rivera had been consistently excellent. Many baseball experts considered him the greatest relief pitcher of all time, particularly when the pressure was on in the postseason. But this time, Rivera ran out of gas. Arizona scored twice to win the game and the series.

DEREK JETER

CHASING NUMBER 27

The loss to Arizona shattered the air of invincibility that had surrounded the Yankees for five years. Suddenly, the Evil Empire seemed less threatening to the rest of the AL. The Yankees continued to dominate the AL East, winning five straight division titles between 2002 and 2006 and earning a Wild Card berth in 2007. New York faltered in the playoffs, however, reaching the World Series only once (in 2003). That

EXTRAORDINARY ENDINGS

The 2001 World Series between the Yankees and Arizona Diamondbacks featured some eerie events. The Diamondbacks started quickly, winning Games 1 and 2 at home behind pitching aces Curt Schilling and Randy Johnson. The teams went to New York for Game 3, and emotions ran high. Fans cheered and cried as a flag that had flown at the World Trade Center on September 11 was displayed, and the Yanks managed a narrow 2–1 victory. In Game 4, which took place on Halloween, the Diamondbacks led 3–1 with two outs in the ninth before Yankees first baseman Tino Martinez hit a two-run homer off Arizona reliever Byung-Hyun Kim to tie the contest. One inning later, as the clock struck midnight, Derek Jeter homered to give the Yankees the win. Most Yankees fans believed that comeback could not be equaled. But, incredibly, the same thing happened the next night; this time, third baseman Scott Brosius hit a game-tying homer off Kim in the ninth, and the Yankees won in extra innings again. The Yankees' magic ended when the teams returned to Arizona, though. Johnson dominated New York's batters in Game 6, and the Diamondbacks staged their own dramatic comeback to win Game 7 and claim the championship.

RIGHT FIELDER · BABE RUTH

Excitement accompanied Babe Ruth wherever he went. "When he entered a clubhouse, a room, or a ballfield, there seemed to be flags waving and bands playing constantly," said Yankees pitcher Waite Hoyt. Ruth's appetite for food was matched only by his appetite for admiration, and his fans loved the "Sultan of Swat" for his powerful swing and playful personality. The Babe was the highest-paid player of his era and felt he deserved every penny. When a reporter once asked Ruth why he should earn more than the president of the United States, Ruth replied, "I had a better year than he did."

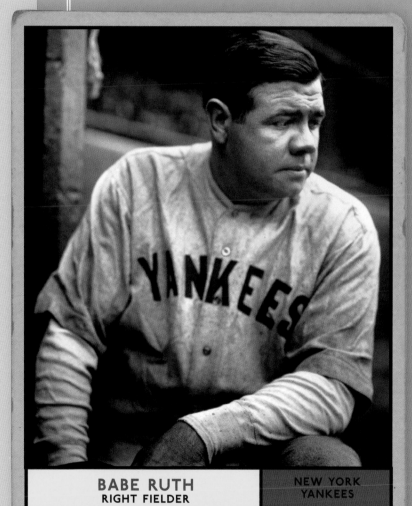

BABE RUTH
RIGHT FIELDER

NEW YORK
YANKEES

STATS

Yankees seasons: 1920–34

Height: 6-foot-2

Weight: 215

- **714 career HR**

- **2,217 career RBI**

- **.342 career BA**

- **Baseball Hall of Fame inductee (1936)**

MANAGER · JOE TORRE

When Joe Torre was first named manager of the Yankees, many New York fans were unhappy. Torre had previously managed in St. Louis, Atlanta, and New York (with the Mets) and had had limited success. But the Brooklyn native quickly changed Yankees fans' opinions by winning a world championship in his first year at the helm. At the ticker-tape parade that followed the big win, Torre commented, "Maybe the Good Lord was just waiting for me to put on the pinstripes." In Torre's 12 years of guiding the Yankees, his clubs won 1,173 games and reached the playoffs every year.

JOE TORRE
MANAGER

NEW YORK
YANKEES

STATS

Yankees seasons as manager:
  1996–2007

Managerial record: 2,326–1,997

World Series championships:
  1996, 1998, 1999, 2000

time, the Florida Marlins upset the Yankees in the "Fall Classic" and prevented them from wearing a 27th crown.

Throughout these frustrating years, the Yankees continued to tinker with their roster, signing free agents and bringing up youngsters from their minor-league system. In 2004, superstar Alex Rodriguez, a Gold Glove-winning shortstop with amazing power and the most lucrative contract in baseball history, signed with New York and agreed to move to third base to play alongside Jeter. Rodriguez immediately began slamming the ball out of Yankee Stadium in his pursuit of baseball's all-time career home run record. Joining Rodriguez in the infield was swift second baseman Robinson Cano, while Taiwanese pitcher Chien-Ming Wang and high-energy reliever Joba Chamberlain were added to the pitching staff.

Following the 2007 season, when the Yankees failed again in the playoffs and their archrivals, the Red Sox, won the championship, Torre was replaced as manager by former Yankees catcher Joe Girardi. "He likes to compete all the time, and he's mentally tough," said New York general manager Brian Cashman in explaining why the club chose Girardi. The new skipper showed his intention to win in New York by wearing jersey number 27. Pointing to the number before a gathering of media, Girardi declared, "This is where we want to end up."

It took two years for Girardi to achieve his goal. After the club missed the postseason in 2008 for the first time in 13 years, the Yankees bounced back in 2009. Their success was due in part to Girardi's managerial decisions, such as moving Jeter to the leadoff spot in the batting order and using his pitching staff more effectively. An even bigger factor was the team's signing of three very talented and high-paid free agents—slugging first baseman Mark Teixeira, big left-handed hurler C. C. Sabathia, and right-handed power pitcher A. J. Burnett. The newcomers combined perfectly with their new teammates to create another winning machine in New York.

The Yankees stumbled early in the season. Then Teixeira and Rodriguez began pounding the ball and driving in runs in bunches, Jeter made a season-long charge at the AL batting title, Sabathia and Pettitte consistently shut down opponents, and Rivera was his usual "lights-out" in sealing victories. The Yankees won a major-league-high 103 games and stormed into the postseason. This time, they would not be stopped. They romped by the Minnesota Twins, outfought the Los Angeles Angels of Anaheim, and then dispatched the Philadelphia Phillies in the World Series to claim their 27th world championship.

Even as they celebrated, the Yankees began strategizing for future

PIE IN THE FACE

Early in the 2009 season, the star-laden Yankees were underachieving. Then, on a Friday evening in mid-May, outfielder Melky Cabrera ripped a two-run single in the bottom of the ninth inning to complete an exciting comeback victory over the Minnesota Twins. As New York fans stood and celebrated, Cabrera was being interviewed by a television reporter. Suddenly, pitcher A. J. Burnett rushed toward Cabrera and slapped a whipped cream pie in his face. When Alex Rodriguez smashed a walk-off home run the next night, Burnett struck again with a celebratory pie as the All-Star third-sacker was being interviewed. The pie-throwing amused Yankees fans and seemed to relieve the pressure on the players, and the team began winning more consistently. Burnett told reporters, "I didn't know if I should throw the pies or not. Were things like that done at Yankee Stadium? But I decided to go for it." The Yankees staged 11 more dramatic, final-inning victories during the regular season and playoffs, and each walk-off hit was celebrated with a pie in the face of the game's hero, compliments of Burnett. By year's end, the Yankees had won another AL pennant and their 27th world championship—thanks, in part, to a pie in the face.

[43]

ROBINSON CANO

Robinson Cano emerged as a big-time star in 2010, batting .319 with 29 homers and 109 RBI and playing solid defense at second base.

INDEX